To my dear P.A.S.J.A.
– Ellen

To my three little adventurers.
May you always stay curious.
– Anna

Copyright © 2022 Clavis Publishing Inc., New York

Visit us on the Web at www.clavis-publishing.com.

Flip, Flop, to the Beach We Go written by Ellen DeLange and illustrated by Anna Lindsten

ISBN 978-1-60537-716-2

This book was printed in November 2021 at Nikara, M. R. Štefánika 858/25, 963 01 Krupina, Slovakia.

First Edition
10 9 8 7 6 5 4 3 2 1

WRITTEN BY ELLEN DeLANGE
ILLUSTRATED BY ANNA LINDSTEN

FLIP FLOP
TO THE BEACH WE GO

Clavis
NEW YORK

Sunrays shining through the window,
slowly we're opening our eyes.

Yippee! Great day for a beach adventure, the weather is already looking very nice.

Dressing up in breezy summer clothes,
wait, don't forget our hat.

Water, sunscreen, bucket, and ball.
Check! We're all set.

Krrrr, krrrr,
squeak the wheels of our little car.

Everything on board?
Off we go, it's not that far.

Crunch, crunch, giggle, giggle,
sand tickling underneath our feet.

The sun is getting warmer now,
our umbrella protects us against the heat.

Splash, stomp, splash, stomp,
jumping like dolphins, over a wave.

Collecting shells for hermit crabs,
keeping them cool and safe.

Splash, spatter, splash, spatter,
fishes trapped in a tidal pool,
we have to set them free.

Carefully catching them in our net,
bringing them back to the sea.

Shovel, swoosh, shovel, swoosh,
building a castle with our bucket and spade.

Perfect place for starfish to hide
and to find some shade.

Slush, slush . . . slush, slush . . .
footprints in the muddy sand,
they don't stay for long.

When we turn around to look,
they're already gone.

Squawk, squawk,
dog is chasing seagulls
along the shore.

Bark, bark, birds fly up,
come back here and play
some more.

Whoosh, whoosh, goes the wind,
kites are flying high.

Look what else is flying there,
so high up in the sky.

Oh, oh, there goes our ball,
up and up and up . . .

Together we run, as fast as we can,
jumping high, we're in luck!

Tinkle, tinkle, ring, ring,
that's a familiar tone.

Yummy, yummy,
my favorite ice cream,
in a waffle cone.

Bye-bye, seagulls, bye-bye, beach,
it's time to pack.

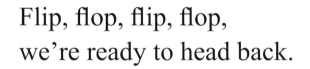

Flip, flop, flip, flop,
we're ready to head back.

Splash, spatter, splash, spatter,
rinsing off all the salt and sand.

What a wonderful day we had,
we even made a friend.

Lantern, book, and fluffy pillow,
ready to camp in our backyard tent.

Reading a bedtime story,
we didn't make it to . . .

THE END . . .